THE
NEPTUNE
FOUNTAIN

The Apprenticeship of a Renaissance Sculptor

written and illustrated by

TAYLOR MORRISON

HOLIDAY HOUSE/NEW YORK

To My Grandparents

Author's Note

While doing research for this book, I looked up Renaissance art on the Internet. A page appeared announcing Luigi Corsanini's Sculpture Workshop. I faxed him a note saying I would like to meet, but didn't really expect a response. Two days later, I received a fax from Luigi saying he would be glad to meet and answer questions.

The Corsaninis fed me wonderful meals and allowed me in their studio. Luigi and his son, Leonardo, explained their work methods with the help of an interpreter named Allesandra. "This takes so long!" I told Leonardo as he showed me how to measure and cut a marble block from a plaster model.

"This is a work of patience, Taylor," he said.

The Neptune Fountain, the Piazza Corsanini in Rome, and the characters in this book are all fictitious.

Library of Congress Cataloging-in-Publication Data
Morrison, Taylor.
The Neptune fountain: The Apprenticeship of a Renaissance Sculptor
written and illustrated by Taylor Morrison. — 1st ed.
p.   cm.
Companion vol. to the author's Antonio's apprenticeship.
Summary: In seventeenth-century Rome, fifteen-year-old Marco is
excited to be apprenticed to a famous sculptor but soon discovers
that he has much to learn before he is allowed to touch a piece of
stone.
ISBN 0-8234-1293-8 (lib.)
[1. Apprentices—Fiction. 2. Sculpture, Renaissance—Italy—
Fiction.] I. Title.
PZ7.M845146Ne   1997   96-41735   CIP   AC
[Fic]—dc20

I was born fifteen years ago today in 1605. My father wants me to continue working with him in the shoe shop, but I want to be like Luigi Borghini, the greatest sculptor in Rome. Today I am going to his studio to ask him if he will take me on as an apprentice.

As I enter Borghini's studio, the smell of cut marble fills the air and white dust covers my shoes. Maestro Borghini stops chiseling and looks down at me. My throat tightens so I can barely speak.

"Maestro Borghini, I am Marco Baicchi. I have no greater wish than to be your apprentice. I brought you this wax model of an archer that I've worked on for weeks to prove I have talent."

Borghini grabs the model, squashes it, and with a few quick movements of his fingers somehow makes my archer seem to strain his muscles pulling the bow.

"I do need a boy to clean my studio," he tells me. "If you are better with a broom than you are with wax, I might be able to teach you to sculpt marble."

While sweeping out the studio, I notice a clay model of a fountain.

"It is a Neptune fountain for the Piazza Corsanini," another apprentice called Lapo explains. "His Holiness the pope held a competition to decide who should create it. All of the finest sculptors in Rome entered models, but naturally Borghini won. You're the new apprentice, aren't you? Do you even know how to chisel marble?" he asks me.

"No," I reply.

"You're lucky," Lapo says, laughing. "Maestro Borghini needs more workers for the fountain. Even a fool like you who knows nothing will do!"

I'll show that wretch I can be a sculptor.

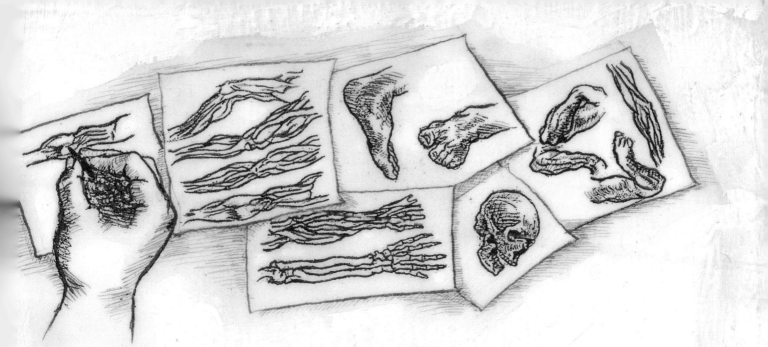

Borghini's studio is a busy and unusual place. Sometimes dead bodies are brought in and dissected. The apprentices draw the bones and muscles to study them. There is also a wooden chest full of Maestro's drawings that I copy for practice.

"Some of these drawings are by my master's hand," Borghini tells me. "In my youth, I spent years copying his drawings at this very table."

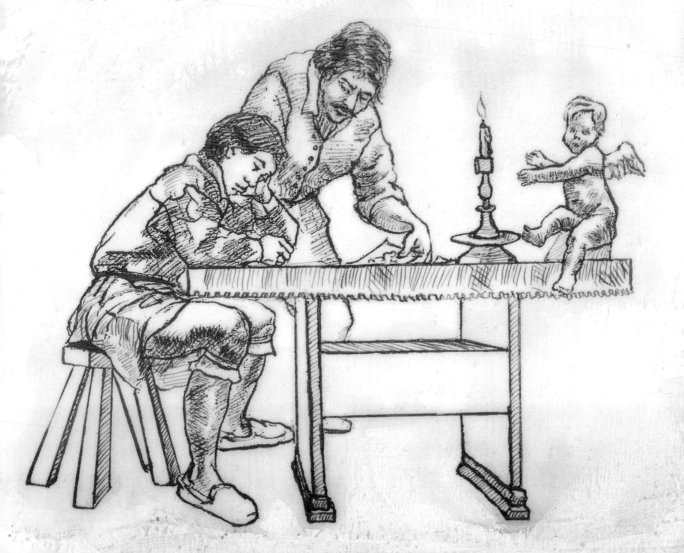

Today after cleaning the studio, Borghini gives me some charcoal sticks and paper. "Go see my friend, Jacopo Bassano. He is a wealthy banker and has a large collection of antique sculptures in his garden. Learn from the ancients how to create beautiful figures. Notice the emotion they put in marble statues," he says before sending me off.

In Jacopo's garden, I am amazed at how the ancients sculpted all kinds of figures so skillfully that they seem alive. When the sun falls below the rooftops, the marble figures lose their glow and I run home for dinner.

In the morning, we help create small models of the figures that will appear in the fountain. First we melt hot wax and stick iron wires into wooden boards to create armatures for miniature wax *bozzettos*. Then Borghini and his best assistants form pose after pose to find the perfect one for the marble figures. They have worked on them twenty days straight, so far. Maestro is pulling his hair out over the Neptunes. He says none of them expresses the god's magnificence.

I was certain that Borghini would never be satisfied with even one of the wax models' poses, but now we are finally ready to make full-sized clay replicas. First we build a wooden armature. Then we tie hay on, so the clay will stick. I mix horsehair into the damp clay to prevent the clay from cracking when it dries. As we place the clay over the wooden skeleton, the figure slowly grows. Before long, I am coated with filthy mud and horsehair. I thought we were making the figures out of marble. I haven't touched one piece yet!

After three months, the clay models are complete. Next, we measure them all in three dimensions with large compasses and carpenter's squares.

"What are the measurements for?" I ask Borghini.

"To find the right marble block. Imagine a clay model buried inside a marble block. If the block is too small, the figure cannot be carved from it. I make sketches that have measurements of the sizes of blocks we need. We trim the blocks at the marble quarry to reduce their weight. Then the cost of shipping them back to Rome is lower. Painters have it easy. They can get materials for their craft anywhere. A sculptor has no such luxury."

Borghini is ready now to send three of us north to Carrara by ship. The best marble is quarried there. Borghini's assistant, Massimo, Lapo, and I will go.

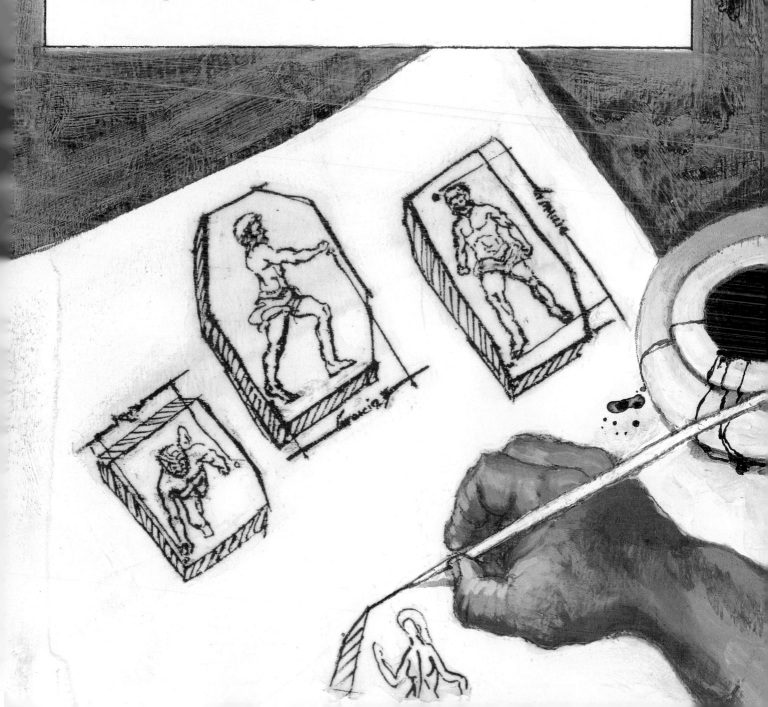

When we arrive in Carrara, we hike up steep mountains to the marble quarries. The quarry workers risk their lives here cutting the massive blocks from the mountainside.

"This marble is called Bianco Carrara," Massimo tells me. "It is strong stone, perfect for large statues standing outside. Maestro entrusts me to inspect the marble blocks for flaws like veins and cracks."

We trim the blocks on the quarry floor. Clang! Clang! Clang! Massimo gracefully swings a hammer against a big chisel called a *scapezzatore*. Large chunks of marble fly off the blocks. When I trim the marble, my hands and arms burn from the long hours of pounding. I want to quit, but then that scoundrel Lapo would call me lazy.

Days after we finish trimming the blocks, we are still waiting for the bad weather to clear. The sea is too violent for the ship to carry our marble back to Rome. When the sky clears, the blocks are finally hoisted by a wooden gin onto the ship. I pray the sea stays calm until we are safely back in Rome with our marble blocks.

At the port in Rome, it takes ten pairs of oxen to pull our cart of marble. On the way to our studio, we pass the Piazza Corsanini where stonecutters working for Borghini are already carving the basin for our fountain. It excites me to imagine that these very blocks will someday be a beautiful sculpture standing right here.

It is a great relief to reach our studio. Even with strong ropes and a windlass, we need all our strength to push each block up on a table next to a clay model. The rafters creak under the tremendous weight. As the massive stone rises above me, I try not to worry about the rope breaking.

"We have raised up the blocks, Maestro; now do we begin carving?" I ask.

"Be patient. New apprentices must learn how much marble is to be cut off the block. The marble figures must match the clay models' proportions exactly." He tells me to listen carefully. "The hand is the outermost point on the front of the clay model. Measure its position carefully. Then mark a point where the hand is to go on the marble block with charcoal. Measure and mark the head the same as you did the hand. Next measure from the hand to the head and mark that distance on the block. Cut away the marble in between until the distance between the point of the hand and head matches that of the model.

"After enough measuring and chiseling with *puntas*, the rough shape of the figure appears from the stone like a person emerging from water." Borghini explains.

"This work takes forever," I complain.

"Quiet, boy!" Borghini hollers. "If you remove too much marble, the block will be ruined. Then I will have to ask the pope to pay hundreds of gold ducats for a new one!'

It is interesting how many sculptors work on one figure. Each has a specific skill. The *panneggiatore* cuts away the rigid marble until the windblown drapery appears.

The *ornatistas* work on the hair. They bore holes with bow drills into the stone head. The holes are enlarged and connected with a chisel to create delicate curls.

Maestro Borghini works on the most difficult parts. He chisels out the basic forms of Neptune's face with his *gradino*, a claw-shaped chisel. He digs intersecting lines into the marble with a sharper-pointed *gradino*. The face gradually grows more defined. It is miraculous to see such graceful hands, feet, arms, and legs emerge from the stone. Day after day the Maestro works without stopping.

Maestro is carefully chiseling the back of a sea nymph when he uncovers a large crack.

"A devil is in my block!" he bellows. "Now I must start over!" He throws down his hammer and furiously scribbles out an order for a new block from Carrara. When his rage ends, Borghini lets me try my hand chiseling a small marble block. I am to carve a grotesque head which will spit water in the fountain. Each day more of the ugly face emerges.

"Lapo, now you must admit I can sculpt marble," I boast to him.

"Well, it figures you can carve hideous things," he jokes. Maestro stares at my sculpture for a moment and then pats me on the back.

After a year and a half of chisel work, the clinking of hammers finally stops. Now the figures are ready to be polished. For months, I rub a rasp and pumice stone over all the surfaces of the marble figures until the stubborn chisel marks are gone.

At last we are moving the sculptures to the Piazza Corsanini. Borghini shouts orders to lift and secure the heavy but delicate statues in place with bronze spikes and rivets. When the work is complete, I stand beside Borghini as we gaze at the veiled fountain.

"Maestro, will I run my own studio someday?" I ask.

"Perhaps, Marco, if you are strong enough to sculpt long days and then stay up half the night studying. Just remember to train your workers as skillfully as you carve marble. It is our duty to pass the art on to others."

It has been three years since we began work on the fountain. As it is unveiled, all of Rome cheers. Our glorious marble figures shine white, glistening in the sun. Underneath them, my marble head proudly spits water. I never imagined it would take so much time: drawing anatomy for hours by flickering candlelight, making scores of models before even lifting a chisel, waiting for marble to arrive from distant mountains, and slowly coaxing figures out of the hard marble blocks. Now I realize that what a sculptor must have above all other things is patience.

GLOSSARY

armature: An internal framework of wire or wood for wax and clay models.

Bianco Carrara *(Bee-aun-co Ca-rare-ah)*: A strong type of marble quarried in Carrara, Italy, used for figurative sculpture.

bozzetto *(bo-zet-o)*: A small model made of wax or clay that a sculptor makes as a study before carving the marble statue.

compass: An adjustable tool with two pointed arms used to measure the proportions of models and sculptures.

carpenter's square: An instrument with two pieces of straight wood joined at right angles used for measuring height.

gin: A large wooden structure used to hoist heavy loads, such as marble blocks, onto ships.

gold ducat: A gold coin once used in Italy.

gradino *(gra-dee-no)*: A fine toothed or clawed chisel used in the final stages before polishing.

Neptune: The Roman god of the sea, who was often used as the main figure in sculptural fountains.

ornatista *(or-nah-tee-sta)*: A sculptor in a studio who specializes in carving hair or ornaments such as jewelry or vases.

panneggiatore *(pan-knee-jeea-to-ray)*: A sculptor who specializes in carving drapery.

pope: The head of the Roman Catholic church. In the seventeenth-century, the pope chose the artists who would create art for public places in Rome.

pumice stone: An abrasive used to make the surface of the marble extremely smooth.

punta *(poon-ta)*: A medium-sized chisel with a point, used for roughing out large forms.

quarry: The place where marble blocks are removed from a mountain.

rasp: A small iron tool with a flat, rough-textured end rubbed on the marble to smooth the surface.

scapezzatore *(sca-pea-za-to-ray)*: A big, heavy chisel used to trim large marble blocks.

stonecutters: Artisans who would carve the stone basin for fountains as well as other architectural elements.

windlass: A wooden machine whose crank wraps a rope around a barrel in order to lift heavy objects.

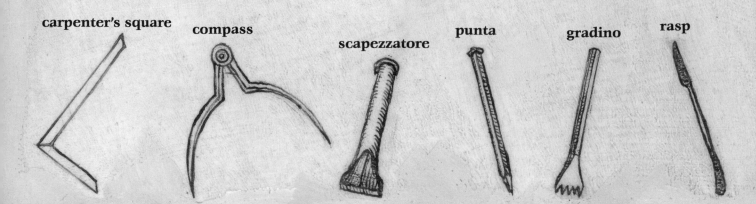

carpenter's square   compass   scapezzatore   punta   gradino   rasp